Donald's Lost Lion

A LEVEL PRE-1 EARLY READER

By Susan Ring

Illustrated by Loter, Inc.

DISNEY
PRESS

New York

Look! There is Mickey Mouse!
Let's play with Donald and Mickey today.
Just say Meeska, Mooska, Mickey Mouse!
Let's go in the Clubhouse.

There is Donald Duck.

Oh, no! He has lost his toy.

It is a lion named 🦁 .
Sparky

He can **ROAR!**
roar

Donald can't go to sleep without him.

We must find 🦁 before bedtime.
Sparky

Here is Toodles! He has come to help.

His tools can help us find .
Sparky

What tools will we use today?

We will use a microphone , a ladder , and a mask .

Where could  be?
Sparky

First, Donald went to the pond.

Maybe  fell into the pond.
Sparky

Which tool can we use to find out?

We will use the  .
mask

No,  did not fall into the pond.
Sparky

Next, Donald went to the park.

Maybe  Sparky went up the tree.

Which tool can we use to find out?

We will use the ladder.

No, Sparky did not go up the tree.

Then, Donald went to the beach.

Look! Goofy is at the beach.

Goofy saw a lion. It had big, green eyes.

The lion made a big ROAR!
roar

Could  be here at the beach?
Sparky

Which tool can we use to find out?

We will use the 🎤 .
microphone

Maybe we can hear him ROAR!
roar

Everybody listens for  .
Sparky

They hear three things.

First, they hear  .
bees

After that, they hear  .
frogs

Then, they hear a  !
monkey

Donald finds a  on the sand.
monkey

What do they hear next?

They hear a ROAR!

It sounds like ![roar] Sparky.

But they don't see ![Sparky].

They see Pete.

Pete has  !
Sparky

Donald is very, very happy.

But Pete is sad.

He lost his best toy. He lost his .
monkey

Donald gives the  to Pete.

monkey

Pete gives  to Donald.

Sparky

Now, everybody is happy.

It is time for Donald to go home.

Good night, Donald.

Good night, .
Sparky

ROAR!
Roar